To unusual friends everywhere

First U.S. Edition 1995
Text and illustrations copyright © 1994 by Rainbow Grafics—Baronian Books
English adaptation copyright © 1995 by Bradbury Press

Bradbury Press
Macmillan Publishing Company
866 Third Avenue
New York, NY 10022

Maxwell Macmillan Canada, Inc.
1200 Eglinton Avenue East
Suite 200
Don Mills, Ontario M3C 3N1

Macmillan Publishing Company is part of the Maxwell
Communication Group of Companies.

Printed and bound in Belgium
Production by Rainbow Grafics—Baronian Books, Brussels, Belgium
10 9 8 7 6 5 4 3 2 1
The Library of Congress number is 94-070884
ISBN: 0-02-775668-8

LEMON WHIP

by Razvan

adapted by Deborah Stupple

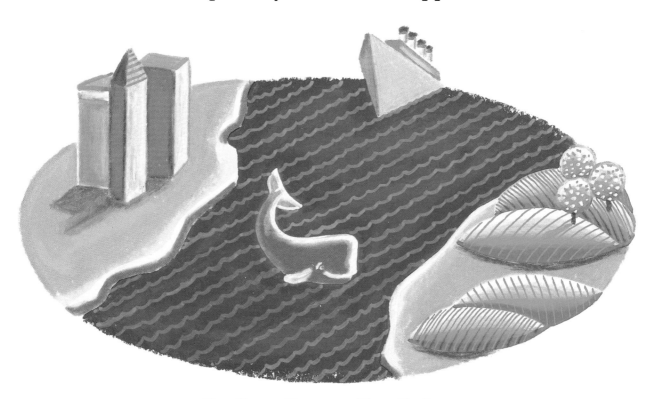

Bradbury Press • New York

Maxwell Macmillan Canada • Toronto
Maxwell Macmillan International
New York • Oxford • Singapore • Sydney

"What a party this will be!"
"No it won't, not for me!"

"Let's both hit the road instead.
Explore the world," the Lemon said.

Beautiful Cake made a shining display,

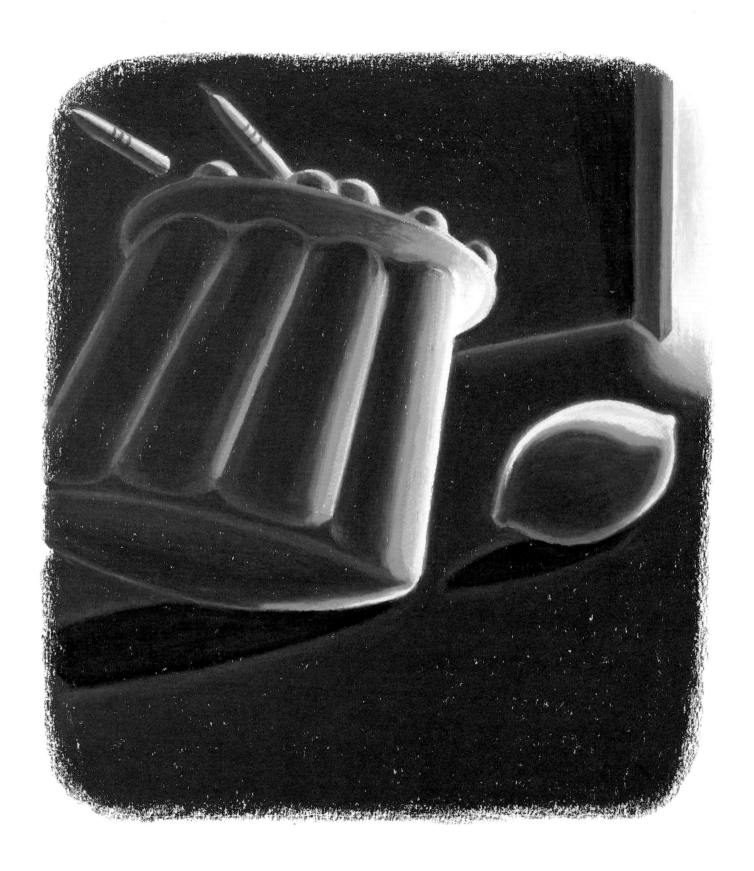

But when the candles went out,
The friends stole away.

Leaving that party table behind

To look for adventures of another kind.

Crossing the street, the pair ducked for cover.

"We're free at last, we have the world to discover!"

Taking to the water, off they float,

With Cake decked out like a brand-new boat.

The flying fish jumped and soared with delight.
"We've never seen such an amazing sight!"

A kind whale taxi took them to shore.
"I hope you find what you're looking for!"

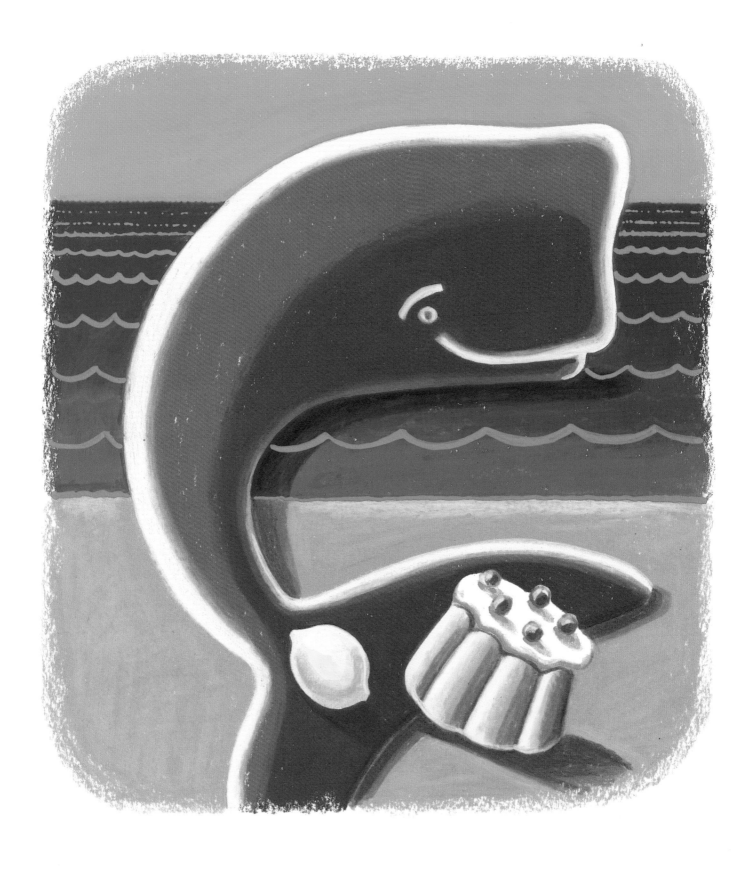

"Good-bye, Mr. Taxi, and thanks for the ride!"

A cart was waiting so they hopped inside.

When they finally arrived,
They got quite a surprise.

A lemon wedding—Here's how we pose
To look our best in the family photos!

"Dancing's such fun when you're with good friends.

I hope this party never ends!"

Before leaving they rested out in the sun.

"You choose where to go," Cake said to Lemon.

"This is the orchard where I was born."

"I love this tree, but it's time to move on."

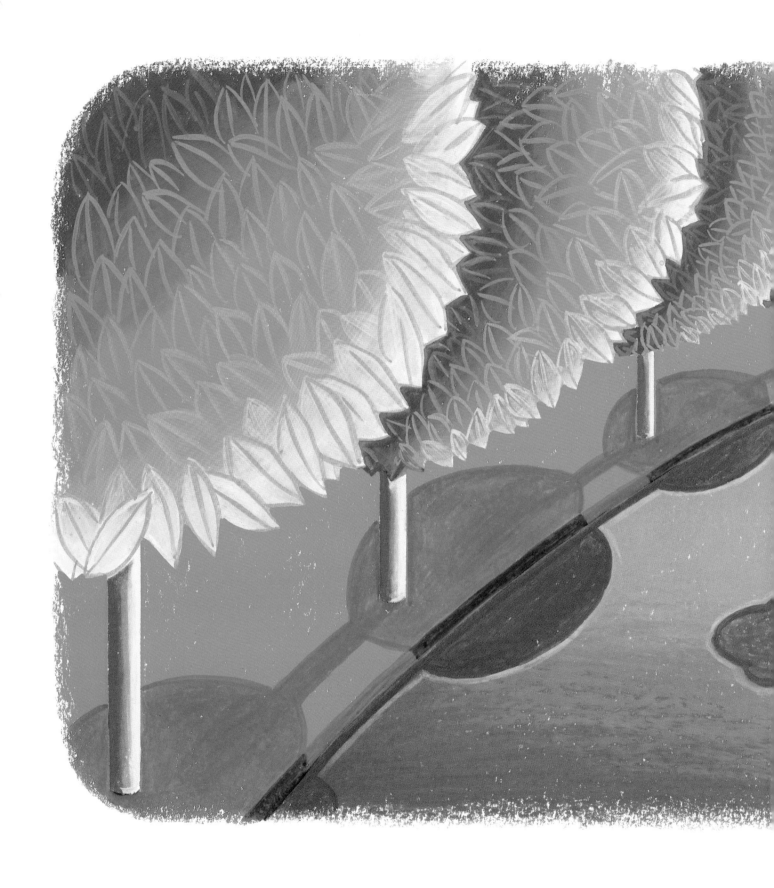

"Let's continue to travel over land and sea."

"Together forever, just you and me!"